THE OFFICIAL ANNUAL 2025

WRITTEN BY STEVE BARTRAM
DESIGNED BY DANIEL JAMES

A Grange Publication

ISBN : 978-1-915879-90-5

CONTENTS

WELCOME TO THE 2025 MANCHESTER UNITED ANNUAL!

To kick off the new edition of your favourite book about the Reds, we relive our 2024 double glory at Wembley Stadium, where both the men's and women's teams won the FA Cup in sensational circumstances!

We also go in-depth on two huge themes of United's history: spectacular goals, where we look back on our greatest-ever efforts in the Premier League, and promoting young talent, where we look into the incredible numbers behind our richest tradition.

Supporting United is a source of huge pride, so we've collated tributes from the players as they spell out their love for the fanbase. There's also a special feature on those in our squads who are living the ultimate dream, as childhood Reds who get to play for the club!

We've also got two exclusive interviews for you: one with new United Women captain and England defender Maya Le Tissier, and another with rapper Headie One, who has been a Reds supporter all his life.

You can expect all of this and plenty more too in the 2025 Manchester United Annual. As ever, your Reds know-how will undergo a serious examination in our quizzes section, after which you can enter our competition to win a signed United shirt!

Enjoy reading and keep the Red flag flying high!

In May 2024, United lifted the FA Cup for the 13th time in club history – capping a wild cup run with an unforgettable win over Manchester City at Wembley Stadium…

WINN3RS

FA CUP WINNERS

THE ROAD TO WEMBLEY

Third round

WIGAN ATHLETIC 0
UNITED 2

(Dalot, Fernandes)

In a one-sided meeting with the League One Latics, United calmly made a winning start to the Cup campaign as Diogo Dalot's first-half curler was followed by a second-half penalty from skipper Bruno Fernandes.

Fourth round

NEWPORT COUNTY 2
UNITED 4

(Fernandes, Mainoo, Antony, Hojlund)

Bruno was among the goals again in Wales, breaking the deadlock early on before Kobbie Mainoo crisply clipped in his first senior goal for the club. The League Two hosts roared back to level, only for Antony and Rasmus Hojlund to fire in late clinchers.

Fifth round

NOTTINGHAM FOREST 0
UNITED 1

(Casemiro)

The Reds' first all-Premier League meeting of the Cup run was a tense affair at the City Ground with little goalmouth action for either side. As extra-time looked certain, however, Casemiro stooped to head in a last-gasp winner!

Quarter-final

UNITED 4

(McTominay, Antony, Rashford, Amad)

LIVERPOOL 3

An all-time classic unfolded as Scott McTominay's opener was overturned by the visitors, only for Antony to force extra-time late on. Marcus Rashford slotted in a second equaliser before, in the 120th minute, Amad sent Old Trafford wild with a brilliant winner.

Semi-final

COVENTRY CITY 3
UNITED 3

(McTominay, Maguire, Fernandes)

United win 4-2 on penalties

For 70 minutes United were coasting at Wembley, with well-worked goals from McTominay and Harry Maguire, plus a deflected Bruno effort. Then, the Championship side bagged three late goals to force extra-time and a penalty shootout, in which the Reds triumphed. Phew!

THE FINAL

MAN CITY 1 UNITED 2

(Garnacho, Mainoo)

In a repeat of the 2023 FA Cup final, United faced Pep Guardiola's Blues at Wembley. This time, however, there was a happy ending as the Reds deservedly triumphed after turning in the performance of the season to bring the trophy back to Old Trafford.

Alejandro Garnacho opened the scoring when he pounced to tap into an empty net after a defensive mix-up between Stefan Ortega and Josko Gvardiol, and United's dream first half peaked soon afterwards when Kobbie Mainoo stroked home following a brilliant team move.

A superb defensive effort from United continued throughout the second half and, although Jeremy Doku netted a late consolation, the Reds held on to record a rousing victory and bag a second major cup in two seasons. Let's go!

FA CUP WINNERS

LOVING IT!

At full-time, United's players were predictably thrilled after the superb Wembley triumph...

“ ”

IT MEANS ABSOLUTELY EVERYTHING.

It's incredible. We knew we had to come together and the staff and players have been amazing. The preparation has been spot on. We've shown we can compete and we can win games. It's such a big win on such a big stage.

Kobbie Mainoo

“ ”

IT IS A SPECIAL FEELING AND THESE FANS DESERVE IT MORE THAN ANYTHING.

It means a lot, winning this trophy. This was a very big step for us. It was more than the game plan; the mentality, you could smell it in the dressing room. In the game we were connected with each other, we were ready like I have never seen this season. Today showed that if we are a team and we have this mentality, we can beat anyone.

Diogo Dalot

“”

IT IS AN INCREDIBLE WIN.

Nobody believed in us but this day, with these fans, is an incredible moment for us. We fought like it was the last game of our lives and we are very happy. The fans are incredible and we have to say thank you to them. Whether we lose or win they are always there, home games or away games and Wembley now.

Alejandro Garnacho

“”

IT IS ALWAYS BEST TO END ON A HIGH.

We have players in the squad with high potential and we are progressing. The FA Cup was a trophy on my bucket list. It is a huge trophy and I am so happy that we won this with the players, team and staff. It was a real team performance. I really enjoyed this final, you saw all the work we put in together.

Erik ten Hag

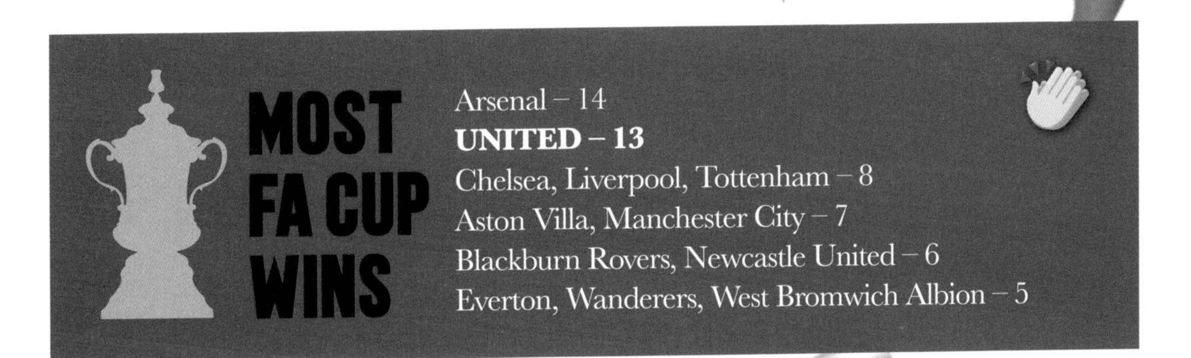

HISTORY

In 2023/24, Manchester United Women took a special place in the record books by winning the Reds' first major honour after overpowering Spurs in the FA Cup final. Here's how we did it...

MAKERS!

THE FINAL

UNITED 4 SPURS 0

(Toone, Williams, Garcia 2)

"What a feeling," grinned Ella Toone, having scored the opening goal of the 2024 Adobe Women's FA Cup final and inspired Manchester United Women to a first-ever major honour.

The Tyldesley-born attacker, who has been with the club since its formation in 2018, blasted in the Reds' goal of the season in first-half injury time, curling an unstoppable effort into the top corner, to set United on course to make history.

By that stage, Marc Skinner's side had already dominated the majority of the game and, having taken the lead, the Reds continued to boss matters at Wembley. Shortly after half-time, veteran striker Rachel Williams headed home a second goal to strengthen United's hold on the game, before fellow forward Lucia Garcia took over.

The Spaniard pounced on a defensive error just before the hour mark to slot into an open goal, then added a superb fourth with 16 minutes remaining to put the outcome beyond doubt. At the other end, a superb defensive performance ensured a clean sheet to wrap up a comfortable win for the Reds and a historic first major trophy.

Having lifted the FA Cup to cement his side's place in club history, boss Skinner quickly turned his sights to the future, promising: "We've got nothing but growth to happen. This is the first of what I hope is many. We've got work to do and let's push on from here."

THE ROAD TO WEMBLEY

Fourth round

UNITED 5

(Toone, Parris 2, Williams, Malard)

NEWCASTLE 0

Fifth round

SOUTHAMPTON 1

UNITED 3

(Toone, Williams 2)

Quarter-final

BRIGHTON 0

UNITED 4

(Turner, Parris, Garcia, Naalsund)

Semi-final

UNITED 2

(Garcia, Williams)

CHELSEA 1

RELIVE THE GLORY

Scan this QR code to watch highlights of United's amazing Wembley win...

HISTORY MAKERS

THIS IS WHAT IT MEANS

United's players were beyond thrilled to help the club make history at Wembley...

"

I'M BUZZING, WHAT A DAY.

Coming in last season [in the 2023 final against Chelsea] and having that taste of what it means to play in a final for your club at Wembley, it made us hungrier than ever today to get the job done. The fans were amazing. We scored some great goals and I'm absolutely buzzing that we're FA Cup winners.

Ella Toone

"

TO LIFT A TROPHY AT WEMBLEY IS A DREAM COME TRUE.

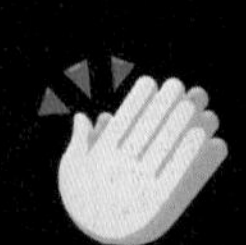

It feels amazing. I've had six years here, the first year in the Championship, and it has always been our aim. Since coming up, we've wanted to win as many trophies as possible and now we've finally achieved it. As soon as the final whistle went, I turned around and saw Millie [Turner] and just thought: wow! Six years in the making. Me, Mills, Tooney and Leah [Galton], the originals, and it just means everything to us.

Katie Zelem

“”

EVERYONE WAS GOING WILD!

There was champagne going everywhere! The girls were so happy to finally get over the line.

Nikita Parris

“”

IT'S SPECIAL.

Winning at Wembley never gets old. We've been brilliant in the FA Cup this year and come together at a really good time. You could feel how much it meant to everyone.

Mary Earps

“”

WE ARE JUST SO HIGH AND WE'RE GOING TO ENJOY IT.

Last year I sat out here [after the 2023 final] and watched Chelsea pick up the trophy and I thought: nah, not next year! And we've won it. These are the days and this is what we want. Hopefully we can bring more silverware to United.

Rachel Williams

24

GOALKEEPER

ANDRE ONANA

BORN - 2 APRIL 1996
NKOL NGOK, CAMEROON

WHAT'S HE LIKE TO PLAY WITH?

"Andre has a big personality, he can play football, he can deal with the pressure, he's really positive, he's a leader. That's the style of Manchester United."

Lisandro Martinez

TROPHY CABINET

3 x Eredivisie league titles *(Ajax)*
2 x KNVB Cup *(Ajax)*
1 x Coppa Italia *(Internazionale)*
1 x FA Cup *(United)*

THE ROAD TO OLD TRAFFORD

Having learnt his trade in the academy of Cameroon legend Samuel Eto'o, Onana left Africa to join Barcelona at the age of just 14. The gifted young goalkeeper spent four years in the world-famous La Masia academy before joining Ajax in search of a quicker route to first-team football. Andre soon excelled with the Dutch giants, saving a penalty in just his second senior appearance, and he established himself as one of the best young stoppers in the game. He first crossed paths with United when starting for Ajax in the 2017 Europa League final, which the Reds won 2-0, and in 2022 he again switched league, joining Serie A's Internazionale and playing a major role in their run to the Champions League final. When Erik ten Hag was looking for a top-level goalkeeper to replace the departed David De Gea in 2023, he saw Onana as the only choice.

MAGIC MOMENT

For a goalkeeper, there's no bigger opportunity to be a hero than when you're facing a penalty. For Andre, that chance came in the last seconds of a Champions League clash with FC Copenhagen in 2023, and the Cameroonian brilliantly swatted away Jordan Larsson's effort to preserve a 1-0 United win with the final touch of the game. Phew!

PHALLON TULLIS-JOYCE

91

GOALKEEPER

BORN - 19 OCTOBER 1996
NEW YORK, UNITED STATES 

WHAT'S SHE LIKE TO PLAY WITH?

"She's a fantastic goalkeeper. The beauty of Phallon is that she wants to raise her game to try and get to the highest of levels, and I think she understands the journey and what she has to do"

Marc Skinner

TROPHY CABINET

1 x Division 2 Feminine title *(Stade de Reims)*
1 x NWSL Shield *(OL Reign)*
1 x FA Cup *(United)*

THE ROAD TO UNITED

Born and raised in New York City, gifted stopper Phallon has come a long way to ply her trade for the Reds. A star player for her high school team, she later studied Marine Biology at Miami University and represented the Miami Hurricanes before making her first move into the professional game with Stade de Reims in France's second tier. After two impressive years in Europe, Phallon returned to the United States with NWSL team OL Reign in 2022 and played her way into the starting line-up, where she came to the Reds' attention. Though her first season in English football was spent largely as back-up to established first-choice stopper Mary Earps, the England international's departure opened the door for the American to step forward and claim a starting place between the posts for Marc Skinner's side.

MAGIC MOMENT

In just her third appearance for the Reds, Tullis-Joyce kept goal in United's League Cup showdown with Liverpool. United led 1-0 going into the second half but came under late pressure, during which time Missy Bo Kearns rocketed a close-range shot towards goal, only for Phallon to produce a stunning reaction save which promptly went viral!

PREMIER LEAGUE SCREAMERS!

Take a look back through the archives to relive the most spectacular Premier League goals United have ever scored…

DAVID BECKHAM v WIMBLEDON, 1996/97

The moment Becks became a superstar came in the low-key surroundings of Selhurst Park on the opening day of the 1996/97 season. Picking up the ball inside his own half, David unexpectedly smashed a shot towards the Wimbledon goal, then watched on as it sailed high over goalkeeper Neil Sullivan and into the net. Iconic.

ERIC CANTONA v SUNDERLAND, 1996/97

In his final season before retirement, the king of Old Trafford served up one of his career highlights in a comfortable win over Sunderland. A three-point turn took him away from two defenders, before he sprinted towards goal, played a one-two with Brian McClair and chipped an unbelievable finish into the far top corner. Magnifique!

WAYNE ROONEY v NEWCASTLE UNITED, 2004/05

One of the hardest hits Old Trafford has ever seen. While arguing with the referee over a decision he disagreed with, Wazza kept one eye on the play which was ongoing around him. Then, when the ball dropped his way from a clearing header, he cracked a volley of incredible power high into the top corner of the Stretford End net.

PAUL SCHOLES v ASTON VILLA, 2006/07

A goal only Scholes could score. After a right-wing corner was cleared high into the air by a Villa defender, the Reds' midfield genius opted to take on a first-time volley from fully 25 yards. Few would hit the target from there, but Scholesy's rocket hurtled against the underside of the crossbar and into the net. Good luck finding a cleaner strike!

CRISTIANO RONALDO v PORTSMOUTH, 2007/08

In the hottest season of his Reds career, Cristiano had already opened the scoring against Portsmouth when United were awarded a free-kick, 25 yards from goal. Despite a massive wall to navigate, Ronny arrowed a sensational effort into the top corner of David James's goal at a disbelieving Old Trafford. The best free-kick in Premier League history? Surely!

PREMIER LEAGUE SCREAMERS!

WAYNE ROONEY v MANCHESTER CITY, 2010/11

Of all the club-record 253 goals Wazza scored for United, this will always be the best. Nani's right-wing cross took a deflection, wrong-footing City defender Vincent Kompany, while Rooney reacted far sharper. Leaping into the air, United's no.10 executed a stunning bicycle kick which flew into Joe Hart's goal and into Old Trafford folklore.

ROBIN VAN PERSIE v ASTON VILLA, 2012/13

Dutch superstar van Persie capped a dream debut season with United by wrapping up the Reds' 20th league title in the ultimate fashion. He scored all three goals in a title-clinching 3-0 win over Villa, the second being an all-time classic: a jaw-dropping angled volley which sped into the far corner, following a sublime Wayne Rooney cross-field pass.

EDINSON CAVANI v FULHAM, 2020/21

In supporters' first game back at Old Trafford since the Covid pandemic, Uruguayan goal machine Edi marked the occasion with a moment of brilliance. Latching on to David De Gea's long punt, the brilliant forward drove an incredible 40-yarder over Fulham goalkeeper Alphonse Areola to send the crowd wild in celebration.

ALEJANDRO GARNACHO v EVERTON, 2023/24

Over a decade on from Rooney's overhead cracker against City, Garna produced a moment of equal – arguably greater – brilliance to open the scoring at Goodison Park. Diogo Dalot's deep cross sailed behind the Argentina international, prompting him to spin, leap and smash a mind-blowing overhead kick past Jordan Pickford. A moment of pure wonder.

BRUNO FERNANDES v LIVERPOOL, 2023/24

Our captain is renowned for his speed of thought, which he demonstrated brilliantly during 2024's meeting with Liverpool at Old Trafford. A misplaced pass suddenly presented him with the ball inside the centre-circle and, without hesitation, Bruno simply powered a 40-yard shot straight into the bottom corner... and how we enjoyed it!

LISANDRO

DEFENDER

MARTINEZ 6

BORN - 18 JANUARY 1998
GUALEGUAY, ARGENTINA

WHAT'S HE LIKE TO PLAY WITH?

"Licha's unbelievable. You can see that everyone loves him, the fans love him. His left foot is unbelievable. He's fitted in really well with his aggression and passion, and he can keep getting better and better."

Luke Shaw

TROPHY CABINET

2 x Eredivisie league titles *(Ajax)*
1 x KNVB Cup *(Ajax)*
1 x League Cup *(United)*
1 x FA Cup *(United)*
1 x World Cup *(Argentina)*
1 x Copa America *(Argentina)*

THE ROAD TO OLD TRAFFORD

It didn't take Martinez long to become a fans' favourite at Old Trafford, but the journey to United was far from quick and easy! Born and raised in the humble surroundings of Gualeguay, a small, working-class city, he moved away from home at a young age to pursue his dream of making it big in football. After spells with Newell's Old Boys and Defensa y Justicia, he caught the eye of Ajax and moved to the Netherlands at just 21 years old. Though his first season in Dutch football was disrupted by the 2020 pandemic, he soon established himself as a key player in Erik ten Hag's team and played a major role in Ajax's dominance over the coming seasons. When Ten Hag moved to United in 2022, he quickly signed Licha as a priority, and the newcomer immediately became a crucial part of the squad. Great signing, gaffer!

MAGIC MOMENT

Having missed much of the 2023/24 season with injury, Licha ended the season on a high note by starting the FA Cup final against Manchester City and blunting the Blues' attack throughout. The Argentina star's performance was so good that Pep Guardiola stressed afterwards: "He made the difference in this game."

MILLIE

TURNER

DEFENDER

21

BORN - 7 JULY 1996
WILMSLOW, ENGLAND

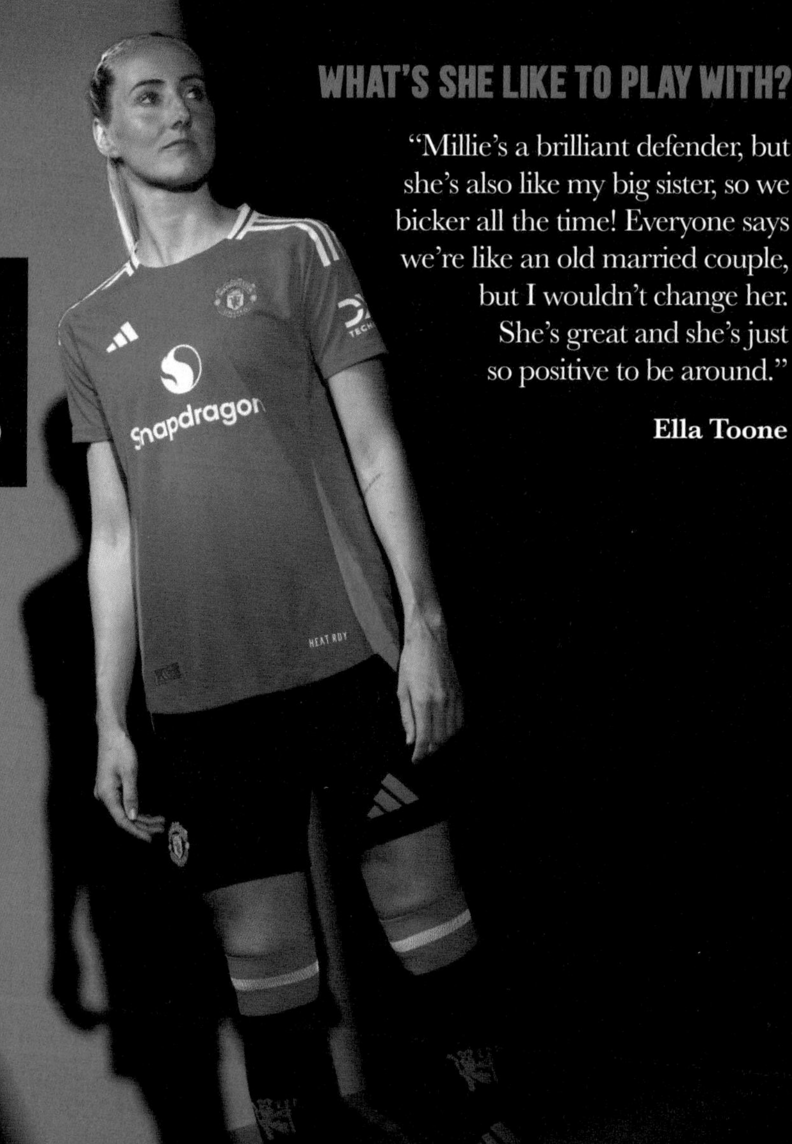

WHAT'S SHE LIKE TO PLAY WITH?

"Millie's a brilliant defender, but she's also like my big sister, so we bicker all the time! Everyone says we're like an old married couple, but I wouldn't change her. She's great and she's just so positive to be around."

Ella Toone

TROPHY CABINET

1 x FA Women's Championship *(United)*

1 x Women's FA Cup *(United)*

THE ROAD TO UNITED

Growing up in nearby Wilmslow, Old Trafford was never far from Millie Turner. She joined up with the Reds' youth system as a teenager after turning down the opportunity to join other major clubs. As her dedication to forging a career in football grew, however, the absence of a professional United team meant that she moved over to Everton, where she rose through the ranks and spent three seasons before moving to Bristol City, who quickly made her captain for her obvious leadership qualities. When United formed professionally ahead of the 2018/19 campaign, however, there was no way Millie could turn down the chance to return to the Reds, and she immediately became a favourite among both fans and team-mates for her no-nonsense style of play and larger-than-life character around the club.

MAGIC MOMENT

The Reds' sterling 2022/23 campaign included a last-gasp win over Aston Villa during the title race run-in, and it was Millie who provided it in some style, thumping home a brilliant injury-time header to send the travelling United fans wild with delight.

REDS IN THE RANKS

For any young United fan, the ultimate dream has always been to pull on that famous shirt and represent the Reds. For some, that dream comes true – not least in our current squads. Across the men's and women's team, there are actually eight childhood United fans in the ranks!

KOBBIE MAINOO

"Manchester United is the club I've always supported. Growing up, watching them, it's just a dream come true to be around it and play for such a big club. I'll play anywhere on the pitch for United."

JAYDE RIVIERE

"I really love the club. I've been a Manchester United fan for as long as I can remember. My dad is the biggest United fan of all. Growing up, watching all those games, Old Trafford was the stadium you wanted to be part of."

BRUNO FERNANDES

"Because of Cristiano, my dream team in England was United. When I was a kid, I had this vision that one day I would play for United. Obviously, every kid born in Portugal during the era of Cristiano and the 2004 Euros and the 2008 Champions League probably had this same crazy dream. But for me... how can I say it? It wasn't crazy. I looked at it like it was just a step on a long journey. A very, very long journey. But I was not going to stop until it happened. So, when my agent called me and told me that United wanted me, it was dream complete."

GABBY GEORGE

"I think the amount of fans that we have
here at Manchester United compared to other
clubs is massive. I came from Everton and
I appreciate my time there, but I think the
fans at Manchester United will always be
the best fans because I'm one of them! As
a massive United fan, I'm buzzing to be here.
It's the club I've supported since I was
born. This club means a lot to me and my
family, and it's where we want to be."

REDS IN THE RÄNKS

JONNY EVANS

"I was a Manchester United fanatic growing up. When I really got engrossed was that 1999 [Treble-winning] season when everything took off. I was 10 or 11. I went down to my auntie's house to watch the Champions League final and my dad was at the pub with his mates watching the game. I can remember as soon as the final whistle went, everyone was on the street kicking the ball pretending to be this player or that player! I remember my dad came and woke me up in the middle of the night. He was like: 'Is that not the best night of your life?!' I always remember him saying that. And it was, at that time, being a Manchester United fan and witnessing that."

ELLA TOONE

"Cristiano was my idol growing up and he still is now. I used to sit on the laptop and Google and YouTube Cristiano Ronaldo doing skills and then I'd do them in the back garden. I always wore his boots and I always wore the number seven shirt when I was growing up. For me, it's been my childhood club, growing up supporting them, going to games at Old Trafford, so it's been amazing to play for the club and even seeing my face on the front of Old Trafford!"

MARCUS RASHFORD

"I grew up here. I have played for this club since I was a boy. My family turned down life-changing money when I was a kid so I could wear this badge, to chase my dream of playing for United. People will actually think I'm weird when I start talking about what United means to me. Because if you're not me, then I'm sure it almost sounds fake. But you have to understand, when I was young, playing for United was everything. When something is inside you like that... it's just inside you. Nobody put it there. It's just there. Deep down, when I look around before every kick-off, I'm still a fan. I can't get that out of my blood."

RASMUS HOJLUND

"I want to bleed for this jersey. My father pushed United over my head, and I started following everybody around the club and of course, I was very into Premier League football and everything around it. I kept watching, and Cristiano Ronaldo was my idol when he was playing back then, so I kept following him and I kept following Manchester United. I think one of the first memories I have in terms of watching a game was probably seeing them winning the Champions League [in 2008]. The penalty shootout against Chelsea. It's a little bit surreal, but yeah, I'm part of that team now!"

BRUNO

MIDFIELDER

FERNANDES 8

BORN - 8 SEPTEMBER 1994
MAIA, PORTUGAL

WHAT'S HE LIKE TO PLAY WITH?

"Bruno's creative and very forward thinking. He always wants to play the ball forward and create opportunities early. He's got such a positive attitude, and the vibe he brings to the team is just positive. Even when he does lose the ball or makes a mistake, he's always running, and working to win it back. I think that definitely rubs off on the other players."

Marcus Rashford

TROPHY CABINET

2 x Taca de Liga *(Sporting Lisbon)*
1 x Taca de Portugal *(Sporting Lisbon)*
1 x League Cup *(United)*
1 x FA Cup *(United)*
1 x UEFA Nations League *(Portugal)*

THE ROAD TO OLD TRAFFORD

Growing up in Portugal, Fernandes always knew where he wanted to end up – Manchester United, as he talks about on page 27. Decades later, he's not only here at Old Trafford; he's also United captain and one of the most influential players in the club's recent history. From a young age, Bruno was addicted to football and never stopped playing, soon leading to a move to Boavista. At that point, however, his career path took an unusual turn, as he left Portugal to play in Italy at just 18, joining Novara, Udinese and Sampdoria before returning to his homeland five years later with Sporting Lisbon. There, his magical talents began dominating the Portuguese league and major clubs began circling around him, leading to United's move for him in early 2020. Vision accomplished!

MAGIC MOMENT

Though lifting two major trophies as captain is a truly major accomplishment, it's tough to imagine a sweeter moment than Bruno's sensational effort against Liverpool in 2024. A first-time effort, from the centre-circle, against our biggest rivals, at the Stretford End? It doesn't get much better than that!

LISA

NAALSUND

MIDFIELDER

16

BORN - 11 JUNE 1995
BERGEN, NORWAY

WHAT'S SHE LIKE TO PLAY WITH?

"Often, a lot of Lisa's work goes unnoticed, but she has a really important role in the team and she's really enjoyable to play alongside."

Katie Zelem

TROPHY CABINET

2 x Toppserien league title *(SK Brann)*
1 x Norwegian Women's Cup *(SK Brann)*
1 x Women's FA Cup *(United)*

THE ROAD TO UNITED

Prior to joining United in 2023, Norwegian international midfielder Lisa spent her entire playing career in her native Norway. In her early years, she was also excellent at handball, but ultimately chose football as her career of choice, thankfully! She spent all of her youth career with Tertnes in Bergen before moving across the city to join Arna-Bjornar, where she made her full league debut at the age of just 16! She immediately became a first-team fixture over the next three seasons, capturing the attention of Sandviken (later renamed as SK Brann), who signed her in 2019. It was there that Lisa's career really took off, as she was named in the league's team of the season, then played a starring role in her side's first league title, a feat followed by the club's first league and cup double in the next campaign. It was no surprise, then, that United soon came knocking!

MAGIC MOMENT

For a player whose main role is governing what happens in midfield, Lisa doesn't score too regularly. As such, it was an unforgettable afternoon for her when the Reds beat Bristol City 2-0 in March 2024, and she scored both goals! "That was very fun," she laughed. "I'm not used to scoring!"

EXCLUSIVE INTERVIEW

MAYA LE TISSIER

At just 22 years old, Maya is already a key player in United's defence, and was named captain in the summer of 2024. Here, the England starlet discusses representing the Reds, her contract extension and her sassy on-field persona!

#1

Maya, thanks very much for your time. Let's start with a big question: what does it mean to you to be a Manchester United player?

It's mad! It's still the case now, but especially when I first came, just before I was about to sign, I just felt like, woah! Just the feeling of signing was heavy. It's obviously a massive club to represent, but for me whenever I put the shirt on, I love that feeling of how big it is. I enjoy it. The pressure can bring out the best in you. It's honestly one of the biggest clubs in the world and there's responsibility on us to put the club where it belongs, competing with the best, and it's only us who can do that out on the pitch. We always try our best and the culture of the club is something that we need to push on now.

#2

Growing up on the island of Guernsey, you had to put in a lot of hard yards to build a career in England. You're representing United and England now, but did that seem like a possibility when you were younger?

The main thing for me was always to come over here and play in the WSL. I suppose that if I'd thought when I was younger that playing for United was my aim, I think that would have been a very big ask. I just wanted to play in the WSL. Signing for Brighton and doing that was amazing, I had a great time down there, but when an opportunity like playing for United comes along, you just can't say no. You take that opportunity with both hands.

EXCLUSIVE INTERVIEW MAYA LE TISSIER

#3 What mindset have you needed to come this far in the game?

I think you have to take everything in your stride. There's obviously a lot of noise around. For me, back on the island I'm from, there's a lot of noise about me playing for United because the main fanbase there is United. Everyone's always thinking about United, following our results. If I sit and think about it in terms of my goals when I was younger, then it's crazy to be here, but it's just something you have to take in your stride and accept that it's your job.

#4 If you had to give one piece of advice to any younger readers who hope to make a career in football, what would it be?

It's hard to say, but when I was younger I wouldn't listen to coaches who would say: "You're doing too much, you can't do this, can't do that." Nah. I would do whatever I could; whatever I knew my body could take, so that I could get to the highest level I could possibly reach. I was not going to let anyone tell me what I couldn't do, just because they were going off data and all that. I was just like, whatever. I was always playing football. Always. It's all that was on my mind. So do what you want to do and what you need to do to get there. Honestly.

#5 During 2023/24, you signed a new contract with United – how excited are you for the future?

I signed a long contract when I first came, so when the offer of another one came along I thought: why not?! When the club want to keep you, that means a lot, and I feel like I can be a big leader and a big part of the team here to push us forward and get us to the top. I wanted to stay here, show my commitment to the club and show that I'm here for the long run. I feel very settled. Literally from the first few weeks here, everyone was taking care of me, and that's one of the main things that struck me when I came in: it's a club where everyone takes care of you. Quite a few of the men's players have jobs here as staff since they've retired, and I think that's nice. It says a lot about the feel of the club and I do feel very settled here.

#6 Although you're still young, you're very mature – what are you like in the dressing room?

Some of the girls say I've got a bit too sassy, but I think I've just come out of my shell a bit more! In the dressing room I'm always having a chat, having a good laugh and I think that's my main thing: laughing at everything that's going on. When I get on the pitch, I'm very competitive and hold very high standards, and I think it's that competitive side which maybe the girls think is me being sassy!

#7 Give us some insight into the dressing room – what's the dynamic like in there?

There have been some real changes as the team has grown and players have arrived who don't speak English as their first language. It has been different and interesting; it's nice that we can involve all the different cultures. It has been really, really good. Everyone brings their own energy to the team in good times and difficult times. The main characters are always Millie [Turner], Rach [Williams], Aoife [Mannion]... the loud ones are funny and come out with crazy stuff. I feel like it's a nice dynamic between all the girls. Everyone brings something. Hinata [Miyazawa] did so, so well. She's so good at English and can understand virtually everything now, whereas at the start we were all walking around with our phones to use translation apps. Geyse's always trying to put on her own music and dance around the changing room, and everyone is like, "what is this?!". Melvine [Malard] is always coming in and saying that the English players have no style, but one time she came in wearing a bright, bright yellow tracksuit, so that speaks for itself! But it's nice having those different cultures.

#8 Finally, United fans are renowned for their support – tell us what it means to have their backing...

Unreal, especially when we're digging deep in games. I'll always remember the FA Cup semi-final against Chelsea last season, when they were insane. It was so nice for us to get it over the line for the fans and for your family too. It's nice that they're all there. It's a massive club, the fans are with us all the time and a lot of the time when we're playing away it feels like a home game because we've got so many fans there. It's more than the home support sometimes, so it can get crazy. It's not normal to have that. The fans are a big part of this team and we're always trying to make them happy and getting the FA Cup for them was a great feeling.

KOBBIE

MAINOO

MIDFIELDER

37

BORN - 19 APRIL 2005
STOCKPORT, ENGLAND

WHAT'S HE LIKE TO PLAY WITH?

"Kobbie is comfortable with the ball and never makes a mistake. For his age he has so much quality. He sees things before others. He's a big talent. I saw him play for the Under-18s two or three years ago, but we didn't know he was going to be this talent and this player."

Bruno Fernandes

TROPHY CABINET

1 x FA Cup *(United)*

THE ROAD TO OLD TRAFFORD

A true United hero even as a teenager, Mainoo oozes class and likeability, and has ever since he first came to the Reds' attention as a six-year-old. "As a young boy, Kobbie was very much as he is today," says Nick Cox, head of United's Academy. "All his team-mates love him. He's very laid back, humble, respectful, but with this steely focus and determination." As he grew and rose through the Academy's ranks, it didn't take Mainoo long to establish himself as a top prospect for the future, and he was tipped for the first team long before he played a major role in the Reds' successful FA Youth Cup campaign of 2022. The clamour continued to build until his breakthrough season in 2023/24, which ended with an FA Cup final winner and a starting slot in England's run to the Euro 2004 final. He's done so much already, but there is a sense that Kobbie is only just getting started...

MAGIC MOMENT

Born and raised a Red, bagging a Wembley winner against Manchester City can hardly be topped. For Kobbie, his FA Cup final decider against the Blues was even sweeter for being an incredibly calm finish at the end of a stupendous team move. An instant all-time classic.

HINATA

MIYAZAWA

MIDFIELDER

20

BORN - 28 NOVEMBER 1999
MINAMIASHIGARA, KANAGAWA, JAPAN

THE ROAD TO UNITED

Japanese international Hinata Miyazawa arrived at United fresh from top-scoring and winning the golden boot at the 2023 FIFA Women's World Cup and, although her first term in English football was heavily disrupted by a broken ankle, she remains one of the most exciting prospects in the WSL. A superb school student, she placed huge importance on her education during her early years as a top footballing prospect, ensuring that she stayed in Japan instead of moving abroad to further her career. While remaining in her homeland, Hini picked up a stack of major honours with Tokyo Verdy Beleza before moving to Mynavi Sendai, by which point she was also studying at university. Her quick thinking is obvious in the way she performs her role as an attacking midfielder, and Hini's supreme intelligence has also allowed her to pick up English at an astonishing rate since her move to United.

WHAT'S SHE LIKE TO PLAY WITH?

"Hinata has fantastic momentum control – the ability to calm everyone else around her. She had some terrible luck getting injured during her first season here, but she's experiencing the physicality of English football and she's learnt a lot already."

Marc Skinner

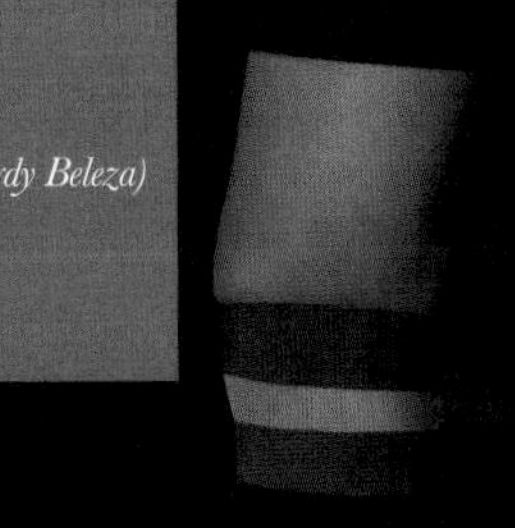

TROPHY CABINET

2 x Nadeshiko League *(Tokyo Verdy Beleza)*
3 x Empress's Cup *(Tokyo Verdy Beleza)*
2 x Nadeshiko League Cup *(Tokyo Verdy Beleza)*
1 x AFC Women's Club Championship *(Tokyo Verdy Beleza)*
1 x Women's FA Cup *(United)*
1 x FIFA Under-20 Women's World Cup *(Japan)*

MAGIC MOMENT

Though her first term at the club was cruelly hampered by injury, Hini did manage to notch her first goal in English football when she powered in a long-range effort to put the Reds ahead at Bristol City in November 2023. It set us up nicely for a 2-0 victory in the WSL at Ashton Gate, with over 14,000 fans there to see it.

Our Greatest TRADITION

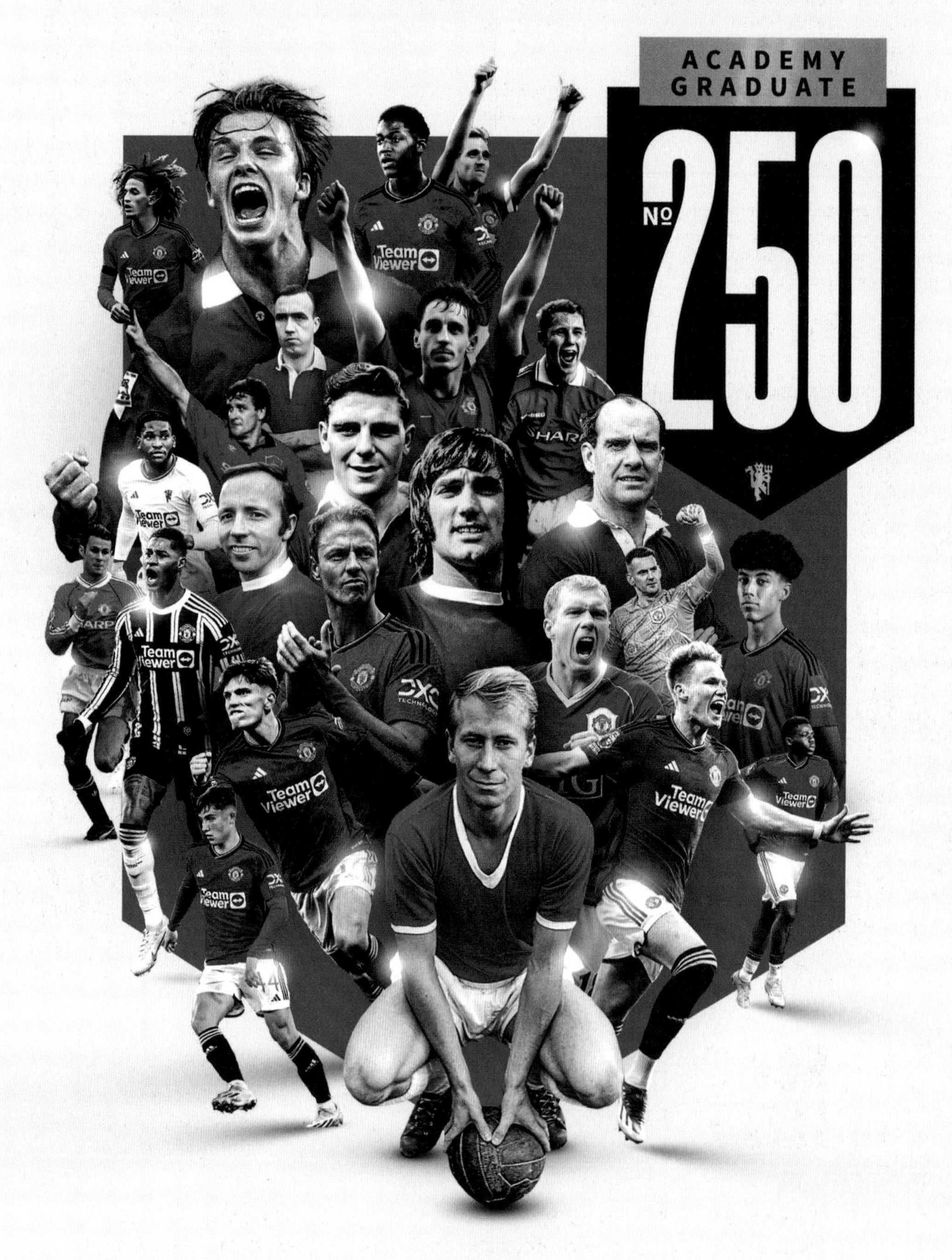

United are renowned for having arguably the best youth system in world football, and the 2023/24 campaign provided further statistical proof…

In 2024, 18-year-old forward **Ethan Wheatley** created an unbelievable statistic as he became the 250th player to come through United's youth system and go on to make a first-team appearance.

Ever since the 1930s, when the club decided to try to develop youngsters into top players rather than constantly make new signings, it has been an Old Trafford tradition to see homegrown talents rise through the ranks and make a career with the Reds or elsewhere within football.

Even as Wheatley made his debut as a late substitute against Sheffield United, he wasn't the only United Academy graduate on the pitch; Scott McTominay and Alejandro Garnacho had trodden the same path as him, as had Blades midfielder Oliver Norwood.

"It's a great club with a massive history, especially in the Academy," grinned Ethan, after the Reds' 4-2 victory. "It's an honour to make my debut and be that number 250. There was a bit of nerves, but as soon as I was stripped and ready to go, I was excited!"

Over time, that same excitement has gripped graduates from 20 countries. While 101 of the 250 come from the Greater Manchester area, some have come from much further afield – even Australia! Between them, they have made over 20,000 appearances, with contributions ranging from a single outing to the club-record 963 held by Ryan Giggs.

As boss Erik ten Hag said: "Everyone at Manchester United should be very proud of our record of producing so many players with the quality and character to represent this incredible club. Strengthening the pathway between the Academy and first team has been one of my priorities as manager, and Ethan is the latest example of this process working well. The opportunity will always be open to those with the right talent and winning attitude to pull on the red shirt."

Here's to the next 250!

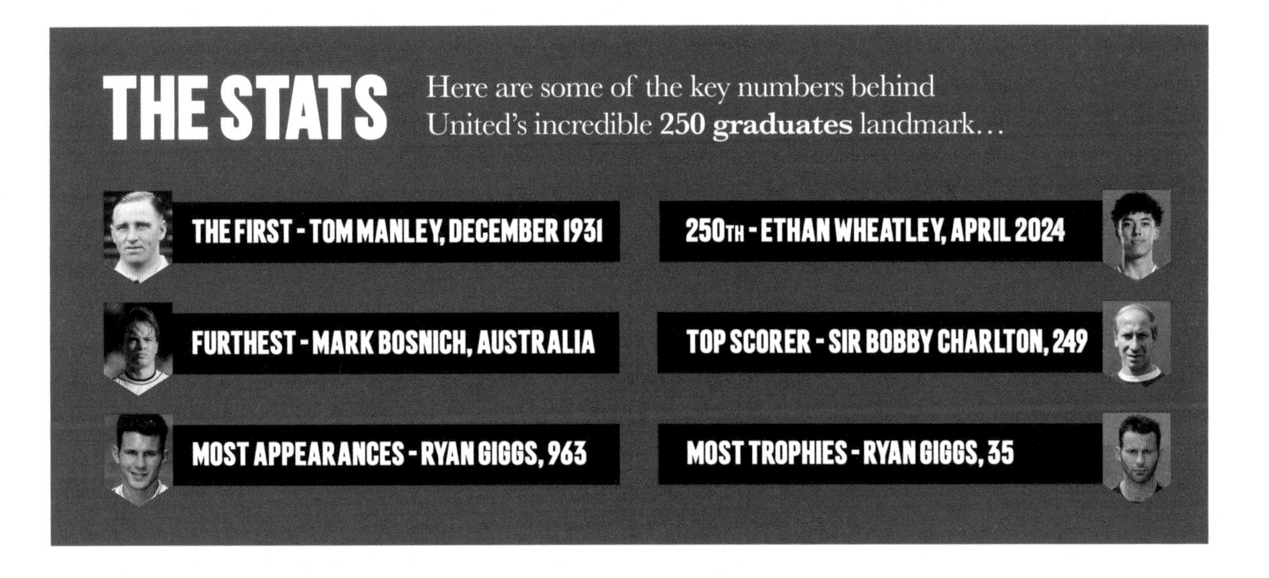

HOW DOES IT FEEL?

For an Academy player like Wheatley, making your first-team debut is one of the greatest moments of your life. Just ask Reds legend Gary Neville...

"I don't think playing football for United is real. You go out and stand in that tunnel and you become something completely different. It's not a normal feeling. It's adrenaline, a buzz, something that comes into your body and you never forget the first time you feel it. I was buzzing after my debut. I'd played for United! From the age of four or five, that had been a dream. After the game I didn't sleep a wink. The adrenaline was still pumping. I just lay there, replaying it all in my mind. My dream had come true."

Our Top 20 Premier League
GRADUATE GOALS

Since the start of the Premier League back in 1992/93, some of United's greatest goals have been scored by homegrown players who came through our youth system. Here's our top 20...

20.

SCOTT MCTOMINAY v MAN CITY (H)

A superb first-time effort from 40 yards to seal a memorable derby win at Old Trafford.

← 8 March 2020

19.

PHIL NEVILLE v SOUTHAMPTON (H)

Despite playing at right-back, the younger Neville brother cracked in a brilliant left-footer.

22 December 2001 →

18.

JOHN O'SHEA v ARSENAL (A)

Sheasy was sent on to defend, but instead clipped home an unreal chip at Highbury!

← 1 February 2005

17.

KIKO MACHEDA v ASTON VILLA (H)

The stuff of dreams, as the 17-year-old curled home a stunning, priceless injury-time winner.

5 April 2009 →

16.

DANNY WELBECK v STOKE CITY (H)

A 30-yard rocket, in off the crossbar, at the Stretford End. There have been worse debuts!

← 15 November 2008

15.

DARRON GIBSON v HULL CITY (A)

The Irish midfielder had dynamite in his boots – as Hull found with this long-range screamer.

24 May 2009 →

14.

JESSE LINGARD v WATFORD (A)

Surging forward from his own half, Jesse wound past several opponents before firing in.

← 28 November 2017

13.

DAVID BECKHAM v WEST HAM (A)

A brilliant ball from Scholesy, followed by an audacious long-range lob from Becks. Perfect!

16 March 2002 →

12.

PAUL POGBA v SWANSEA CITY (A)

A delicious, swiped shot from outside the box – one of the cleanest hits you'll ever see.

← 6 November 2016

11.

RYAN GIGGS v QPR (A)

A brilliant, winding run at full speed, followed by an unstoppable finish. Peak Giggs.

5 February 1994 →

10.

ANDREAS PEREIRA v SOUTHAMPTON (H)

A lightning counterattack, capped by a sensational long-range curler from the Brazilian!

← 2 March 2019

9.

MARCUS RASHFORD v BRIGHTON (A)

After a surging run down the left, Marcus sent Ben White the wrong way twice before finishing!

26 September 2020 →

8.

DAVID BECKHAM v TOTTENHAM (A)

One of Becks' greatest-ever hits – a sublime swerver into the top corner from miles out.

← 12 January 1997

7.

PAUL SCHOLES v MIDDLESBROUGH (A)

Bosh! A joyously brutal first-time hit from Scholesy which hurtled into the top corner.

10 April 2000 →

6.

RYAN GIGGS v TOTTENHAM (A)

Another Giggsy classic: nabbing possession, a cheeky nutmeg and a devastating finish. Oof.

← 19 September 1992

5.

MARK HUGHES v SHEFF WED (H)

One of the hardest half-volleys ever, thrashed in from over 30 yards. Simply unstoppable.

16 March 1994 →

4.

PAUL SCHOLES v BRADFORD CITY (A)

An inch-perfect corner from Becks, met by an equally flawless volley into the bottom corner.

← 25 March 2000

3.

PAUL SCHOLES v ASTON VILLA (A)

An incredible volley which almost cracked the Villa crossbar on its way into the net.

23 December 2006 →

2.

DAVID BECKHAM v WIMBLEDON (A)

The goal which launched a megastar, as Becks bashed one home from inside his own half!

← 17 August 1996

1.

ALEJANDRO GARNACHO v EVERTON (A)

The perfect overhead kick, smashed into the top corner. An all-time great from Alejandro!

26 November 2023 →

WATCH THEM ALL!

Scan this QR code to see the full top 20!

MARCUS

RASHFORD

FORWARD

10

BORN - 31 OCTOBER 1997
MANCHESTER, ENGLAND

WHAT'S HE LIKE TO PLAY WITH?

"I really like and enjoy playing with him. He is a world-class player. He's a player I've looked up to, even though he's only a few years older than me. He has done well since he came in as a 19-year-old and I think he has been a great player ever since."

Rasmus Hojlund

TROPHY CABINET

2 x FA Cup *(United)*
2 x League Cup *(United)*
1 x Europa League *(United)*

THE ROAD TO OLD TRAFFORD

Growing up in Manchester, spending his youth across Wythenshawe, Hulme, Moss Side, Chorlton and Withington, Rashford at times had a tough childhood. "The struggle was real," he later admitted. "It wasn't a commercial. It wasn't a movie. But I wouldn't change any of it, as hard as it was, because it moulded me into who I am." Through it all, his dream was always to represent United, the club he loved. That prompted him to turn down major offers from a variety of clubs even when he was still young. Having been in the Reds' youth system from the age of seven, he eventually signed professional forms in 2014 and never looked back, playing his way to the fringes of the first-team squad before making his senior debut in 2016. After that unforgettable introduction to life in the spotlight, he carried on from there, becoming a first-team fixture and a hero to United fans everywhere.

MAGIC MOMENT

He's gone on to pass 400 appearances and clock up countless memories in United's colours, but a debut brace v Midtjylland is hard to top. A crucial pair at the Stretford End in 2016 made Marcus just the 14th player ever to score twice or more on his Reds debut, and only the sixth youth system graduate. A mind-blowing achievement!

RACHEL

WILLIAMS

FORWARD

28

BORN - 10 JANUARY 1988
LEICESTER, ENGLAND

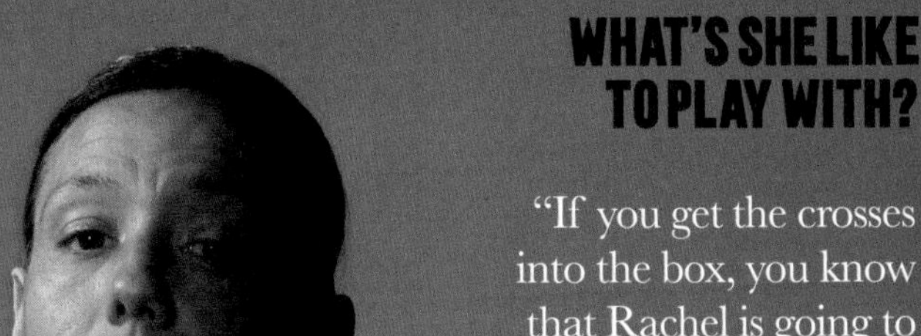

THE ROAD TO UNITED

A powerful, dominant forward blessed with unrivalled experience at the top level, Rachel is an invaluable weapon in the United attack, where her strength, speed of thought and finishing skills have been used to great effect. Having started out before women's football was fully professional, Rach also had a career as a plasterer – a trade which she regards as her real job! She juggled that role alongside her playing career as she rose through the ranks with Leicester City (in two spells), Doncaster Belles, Birmingham City, Chelsea, Notts County, Birmingham again and Tottenham Hotspur before joining the Reds in 2022. By the time of her arrival, she'd clocked up almost 200 WSL appearances, not to mention 13 England caps and a spot in the 2012 Team GB women's football team. If you're looking for a player with a broader range of experiences to lead the attacking line, good luck finding a better fit than Rach!

WHAT'S SHE LIKE TO PLAY WITH?

"If you get the crosses into the box, you know that Rachel is going to be there on the end of them. She's unbelievable in the air and even if three players mark her, you know she's going to get the header."

Ella Toone

TROPHY CABINET

2 x Women's FA Cup *(Birmingham City, United)*

MAGIC MOMENT

Always the player for the big occasion, Rach has come up with a wide range of great contributions when it matters most, but it's impossible to see beyond her superb header in the 2024 FA Cup final, which put the Reds 2-0 up against Spurs and on the road to making club history!

FEEL THE LOVE!

The driving force behind Manchester United is the club's incredible supporters – United is the club's incredible supporters – and that unconditional backing is recognised and returned by United's players and staff…

"Listen, about United supporters, I have so many good things to say. These guys, they are behind us in the good and the bad moments. We feel like, even if it's difficult, we know we have our soldiers behind us."

ANDRE ONANA

"I say it every week, the fans are our 12th player when we're on the pitch. They come out in full force and we appreciate them so much."

ELLA TOONE

"Every time I walk out on to the pitch and I hear the fans singing my name, or I look around Old Trafford before kick-off, I feel that same positive energy."

MARCUS RASHFORD

FEEL THE LOVE!

"Winning feels incredible because our players and our staff have been able to produce it for the best fans in the world. I can't tell you how hard we work every day to do it, and that's for every single fan that loves United."

MARC SKINNER

"The fans have been with us all the way through and they have been amazing, sometimes perhaps when we didn't even deserve it."

DIOGO DALOT

"

Our fans are fantastic. They literally follow us everywhere we go and it's a credit to them and it does not go unnoticed by the players.

"

HANNAH BLUNDELL

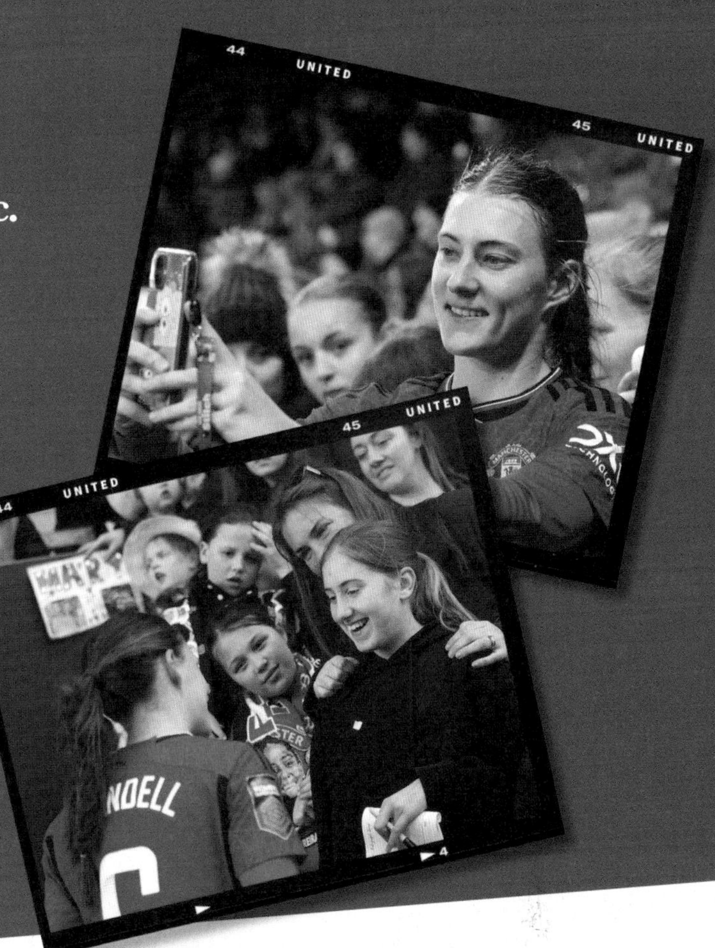

"

Whenever I see someone on the other side of the world wearing my shirt, it gives me such a special feeling. People send me photos from Hong Kong, or from Nigeria, wearing my number 8 shirt, and every single time, it makes me feel so surprised and humble.

"

BRUNO FERNANDES

HEADIE ONE!

Though born and raised in London, rapper **Headie One** is a lifelong United fan. Now, after the release of his latest album, 'The Last One', he tells us exclusively about his memories, his own style of play and fellow Reds in the music industry…

FIRSTLY HEADIE, WHY DO YOU SUPPORT UNITED?

It's funny. I have some cousins who are a few years older than me and they were United supporters, but my dad actually supports Liverpool. [*Laughs*] It's crazy, innit? Because I spent a lot of time with my cousins when I was growing up, from very young, I was infatuated with United. It stuck with me in my childhood and it's carried on from there.

2

YOU WERE BORN IN 1994 — A GREAT TIME TO BE GROWING UP AS A RED. WHAT ARE YOUR EARLIEST MEMORIES OF WATCHING UNITED?

When I was very, very young, my earliest memories would have been seeing Cantona playing, but my more vivid memories are from the early 2000s when we had our rivalry with Arsenal. That's when we had van Nistelrooy, and both Ronaldo and Rooney had just arrived. That's when I really became a proper fan in my own right. The players we had at that time were a joke.

HAVE YOU BEEN ABLE TO GET TO MANY GAMES DOWN THE YEARS?

More recently. When I was younger, Manchester felt like it was so far away – especially to a schoolkid in Tottenham. These days I'm able to go up to Manchester quite a bit for home games. Last season I went to the Crystal Palace away game with my missus. That's the first time I'd been in a United away end and, while it was a sad evening for what happened on the pitch, losing the game, the fans were unreal. It was such a different experience. Even though the team were 4-0 down, everyone kept cheering them on, singing until the final whistle. Crazy.

WHICH HAVE BEEN YOUR FAVOURITE TRIPS TO OLD TRAFFORD?

I can't remember exactly which was my first game because I've been to quite a few, but one of my favourites was beating City 2-1 in 2023 when Rashford scored the winner. That's one of my favourites because the manner in which we won, coming from behind to win late, that was sick.

IN GENERAL, WHAT ARE YOUR FAVOURITE UNITED MEMORIES?

Oh, there are so many. Rooney's scissor kick against City [in 2011] was crazy. Ridiculous. There was a Paul Scholes header in the last second against City [in 2010] as well. One of my favourite games I've watched was the 2008 Champions League final against Chelsea – that's one of my most memorable games, beating them on penalties. That was a proper nail-biter!

DO YOU HAVE FAVOURITE PLAYERS, ALL-TIME AND CURRENT?

Ruud van Nistelrooy, being a striker who scored in nearly every game, that's when it all came together for me. He had this superstar quality about him. In the current squad, I like Rasmus Hojlund a lot, you know. A lot. I like Mainoo. He's a player, man. What a debut season he had, finishing up with the Euros. I like Dalot, whose performances have been sick, but my favourite is Hojlund. He's got a lot about him. I can see him, with a bit more time, being proper good.

BEFORE MUSIC, YOU WERE A PROMISING YOUNG FOOTBALLER UNTIL INJURY STRUCK...

When I was in my school team, I used to play either centre-back or defensive midfield. There was one time where they tried to play me a bit more attacking because we had no-one else to do it at the time, but I always preferred midfield. I wouldn't say I was the best footballer, but one of my strengths was being able to look around and see quite a few things at the same time. That's why that position was good for me. Plus, I wasn't the best at shooting, so seeing things and passing the ball around was better for me.

YOU WENT DOWN A DIFFERENT CAREER PATH, OF COURSE – PRESUMABLY YOU'RE HAPPY WITH HOW THINGS TURNED OUT?

[*Laughs*] It's not turned out bad at all, yeah! I like the fact that I can do what I do and still be a fan as a hobby. It's alright, man!

YOU'VE WORKED WITH STORMZY BEFORE, ANOTHER FAMOUS RED. DO YOU COME ACROSS MANY UNITED FANS IN THE INDUSTRY?

Definitely. There's a few United fans in the industry – but a lot of Arsenal fans as well so we always end up clashing when we have our little discussions. Me and Stormzy had a chat about how things are going at United, I know Dave is a United fan as well and there are a few more too. Definitely too many Arsenal fans in the industry, though!

YOU REFERENCED UNITED IN A LINE IN 'BACK TO BACK' – DO YOU PLAN TO GET IN ANY MORE REFERENCES IN THE FUTURE?

There's one on my new album that's just come out, so I made sure I got one in there!

FINALLY, HAVING WON TWO TROPHIES IN TWO YEARS, HOW OPTIMISTIC ARE YOU FOR UNITED GOING FORWARD?

Definitely very optimistic. I watched the FA Cup final [against Manchester City] in Sri Lanka in some little village, and I was gassed. I can't lie. I feel like, the way things are, if we stay on the trajectory that we're on, then we'll be alright. It can be frustrating at times, but I think that always comes with the process of making something good. Rome wasn't built in a day and we have a lot of positive stuff going on at United. We've got some really big, young players coming through and the future's looking bright.

QUIZZES

How well do you know United? Time to find out by taking on a succession of Reds-based challenges...

WORDSEARCH

Can you find the surnames of the eight players who scored for United at Wembley during 2023/24?

O	G	L	Y	S	R	Y	G	A	N	P	B	G	D	X	Y
H	J	G	G	L	D	B	H	U	Y	A	H	Y	E	N	S
C	W	J	V	Z	W	I	L	L	I	A	M	S	Z	I	C
A	G	N	Q	W	W	W	R	T	O	N	Q	P	K	E	M
N	N	A	Y	H	T	G	E	P	W	F	H	R	T	C	U
R	W	G	R	D	J	W	M	M	V	Q	F	P	T	B	O
A	A	F	Z	C	O	S	F	N	M	Y	S	O	F	O	N
G	N	H	N	B	I	C	Q	Z	F	J	M	R	L	I	U
N	X	Z	U	D	V	A	Q	L	I	I	K	R	I	O	O
L	J	V	E	W	T	F	E	R	N	A	N	D	E	S	A
Q	A	T	E	R	I	U	G	A	M	E	C	V	P	L	E
B	X	O	C	H	J	Q	Y	A	I	U	A	V	R	F	R
T	D	O	O	N	I	A	M	G	S	Y	W	D	F	Q	A
Q	G	N	F	B	Y	T	P	V	C	O	N	Q	S	D	S
M	Y	E	Z	U	D	G	T	N	Q	W	T	E	M	U	G

MCTOMINAY MAGUIRE FERNANDES TOONE
WILLIAMS GARCIA GARNACHO MAINOO

ANSWERS ON PAGE 60